The Dusk Fairy

by Keith Faulkner

illustrated by Helen Cann

Cartwheel
·B·O·O·K·S·®

SCHOLASTIC INC.

New York Toronto London Auckland Sydney
Mexico City New Delhi Hong Kong

The sun was setting and the Dusk Fairy was busy with her
evening work. She was closing all the flowers and making sure
all the little creatures were safe in their beds.

Suddenly, she heard a voice from an open window
just across the meadow.
"Look at this mess! All your toys and clothes are scattered
everywhere!" the voice said. "It's bedtime now, so we
will straighten up in the morning."

The Dusk Fairy listened until she heard the bedroom door close.
Then, with a flutter of her glowing wings, she flew like
a moonbeam to land on the window ledge.

Peering through the glass she could see a little child's face lying on the
pillow. The child had fallen asleep. Quick as a flash, the Dusk Fairy
darted in through the open window to look at the sleeping child.

The bedroom was certainly a terrible mess. Toys and clothes were strewn all over the floor. Pieces of jigsaw puzzles, building blocks, and crayons lay scattered. Dolls, puppets, and books were everywhere.

It would have taken you or me hours and hours to clear up the mess and put everything back in the right place, but we don't have magic like the Dusk Fairy. She just gave a little smile and set to work.

It was just as if a tiny comet or a firefly was zooming around the room while the child quietly slept. Clothes appeared to fold themselves and disappear into drawers or hang themselves in the closet. Books jumped effortlessly back onto the bookshelves.

Toys and dolls flew silently into the toy box, jigsaw puzzles scampered back into their boxes. All the while the Dusk Fairy darted among them, leaving a trail of sparkling stardust behind her. By the time she finished, she was feeling very tired.

When the child's eyes opened in the morning, she thought she was still dreaming. There by her bed was the strangest sight. A little fairy was sleeping with her head resting on the edge of the water glass.

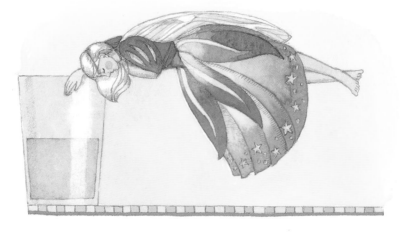

Her body was just floating in the air, gently swaying in the dawn breeze from the open window. The child gasped and the Dusk Fairy awakened. Hovering close to the child's face, she planted a tiny kiss on her cheek before flying out through the open window.

"My goodness! What a wonderful surprise," said Mother as she gazed around the tidy bedroom in amazement. "You must have awakened very early to straighten your room already."

She lifted the child from her bed and gave her a big hug. She was just about to kiss her when she suddenly stopped. "What's this? You seem to have grown a dimple during the night," she said, stroking the child's cheek. "When I was a little girl, we called them fairy kisses."